Nancy Krulik and Amanda Burwasser

Soccer Shocker!

Illustrated by Mike Moran

Sky Pony Press
New York

First Edition

This is a work of fiction. Names, characters, places, and incidents are from the authors' imaginations, and used fictitiously.

While this book aims to accurately describe the steps a child should be able to perform reasonably independently when crafting, a supervising adult should be present at all times. The authors, illustrator, and publisher take no responsibility for any injury caused while making a project from this book.

Sky Pony Press books may be purchased in bulk at special discounts for sales promotion, corporate gifts, fund-raising, or educational purposes. Special editions can also be created to specifications. For details, contact the Special Sales Department, Sky Pony Press, 307 West 36th Street, 11th Floor, New York, NY 10018 or info@skyhorsepublishing.com.

Sky Pony® is a registered trademark of Skyhorse Publishing, Inc.®, a Delaware corporation.

Visit our website at www.skyponypress.com
Books, authors and more at www.skyponypressblog.com

www.realnancykrulik.com
www.mikemoran.net

10 9 8 7 6 5 4 3 2 1

Library of Congress Cataloging-in-Publication Data available on file.

Cover illustration by Mike Moran
Cover design by Georgia Morrissey

Hardcover ISBN: 978-1-5107-1019-1
Ebook ISBN: 978-1-5107-1024-5

Printed in the United States of America

Interior Design by Joshua Barnaby

For my parents, Gladys and Steve Krulik,

higher branches on our family tree

—NK

For my grandparents,

Herman and Lillian Burwasser

—AB

For Kristin

—MM

CONTENTS

1. Bran-Tastic   1

2. Butt Kicks Butt   10

3. Smash!   24

4. Slime Time!   30

5. Something Smells Fishy   38

6. Atomic Flush   50

7. Stinky-buggy-tonsil-toenail-itis   59

8. Poor Wombats   67

9. Do the Wombat Watusi   75

10. Come Clean   85

There's a Soccer Ball
on the Ceiling!   93

1.

Bran-Tastic

"Mom!" I shouted. "Where are the Sugar-Blasted Bubblegum Crispies?"

"We're all out of Bubblegum Crispies," Mom called back from her lab in the garage. "Just pour yourself a bowl of my Fun-with-Fiber Flakes."

"Fiber is healthy for humans," my cousin, Java, said. He was sitting at the kitchen table, speed-clipping coupons for my mom.

Fiber Flakes might be healthy. But they tasted like soggy cardboard. Not that Java would know. Java doesn't eat breakfast.

Java doesn't eat at all.

He doesn't need to. He's an android.

My mom is a scientist. She likes to build things. So she built me a robot cousin.

His name is Jacob **A**lexander **V**ictor **A**pplebaum.

I just call him Java.

Sometimes it's cool having a robot by my side. But other times it can be a real pain.

The hardest part about having Java in the family is I can't tell anyone he isn't human. That's because he's part of my mom's secret project: **Project Droid**.

But keeping Java's secret isn't easy. Especially because he doesn't always act like a normal kid.

"I hate Fiber Flakes," I called to Mom. "Isn't there anything sweet I can have for breakfast?"

"Add some dried fruit," she suggested.

"Dried fruit makes me have to go to the bathroom," I argued.

"Logan, I'm busy," my mother called from the lab. "Just add some dates and nuts to your cereal and eat."

Suddenly Java leaped up from his seat.

"I can do it!" he shouted. He picked up the scissors he'd been using to clip the coupons and began cutting up the calendar on the wall.

"What are you doing?" I asked him.

"Getting dates for your cereal," Java said. "Here's November 17." He dropped the calendar dates into my cereal bowl.

That's what I mean about Java not acting like a normal kid.

I looked down at the paper in my bowl. "I'll have toast," I said.

Just then, Mom walked into the kitchen. At least I *think* it was my mom. It was hard to tell under the helmet and safety glasses.

"Better hurry," Mom said. She dropped her tool kit on the counter. "You two will be late for your soccer game."

Huh?

"What do you mean, *you two*?" I asked Mom nervously.

"Didn't I tell you?" Mom asked. "I signed Java up to be on your soccer team.

You boys are going to play together every Sunday. I think it will be good for Java."

"Soccer is good exercise for humans," Java pointed out.

"But you're not human!" I shouted at him.

"Logan, be nice," my mother scolded.

"It's just that he's always around," I said. "He lives here. He's in my class. And now he's going to be on my soccer team."

"Exactly," my mom said cheerfully. "I think you're doing a great job teaching him how to be human."

I frowned. Mom just didn't get it.

"I don't have time to teach Java all about soccer," I told her. "I'm the team's top scorer. When I'm on the field I have to focus on the game."

Of course, I didn't say that I'd scored only one goal. Or that my goal was against the Lemon-Yellow Lemurs, a team that stunk almost as badly as we did.

"You don't need to teach Java about anything," Mom said. "I programmed all the rules of soccer into his hard drive."

"What if something goes wrong?" I asked her. "You remember the mess he made at the science fair? And this time you won't be there to fix him!"

Saturdays were Mom's only day to clean up her lab. So she never was able to make it to my soccer games.

But that was okay with me.

The last time Mom came to a game was really embarrassing. She called me her Little Bunny Hug and pinched my cheek in front of the other kids on the team.

Top scorers didn't have nicknames like Little Bunny Hug.

"Nothing will go wrong this time," Mom promised. "There are no giant magnets on a soccer field, like at the science fair. There won't be anything to upset his wiring. He'll act like any other kid."

I looked over at my android cousin. He was pulling little pieces of metal from my mother's tool kit and dropping them into the bowl in front of him.

"Look. Now I am adding some nuts to the cereal," he said proudly. "I am adding bolts, too."

I rolled my eyes. *Java, act like any other kid?* Somehow I doubted it.

2.

Butt Kicks Butt

"Those Red Polar Bears are really kicking our butts," I told my friend, Stanley, as we watched the Polar Bears' center forward kick another goal into our net.

"The score is only three to nothing," Stanley said. "We can still catch up. *You* could score a goal for us. After all, you're our team's top scorer."

Team's top scorer. I loved the sound of that.

But the truth was, the fact that I had scored a goal in a game a few weeks ago wasn't helping us now.

"We're already near the end of the second half," I told Stanley. "We're gonna be shut out. And the Silverspoon twins will never let us live it down."

The Silverspoon twins were both on the Red Polar Bears. The Red Polar Bears had kicked our Purple Wombat butts the last time we'd played them. And it looked like they were about to do it again.

It wasn't like the Red Polar Bears were league champs or anything. They just didn't stink as badly we did.

I looked across the field. Jerry Silverspoon was standing in the Polar Bear goal scratching his rear. He had nothing else to do.

No Purple Wombat had gotten close to scoring a goal all day.

"Hey, look!" Stanley shouted excitedly. He pointed to something fluttering off to the side of the field. "There's a buff-bellied hummingbird!"

Bonk! Suddenly the soccer ball bashed Stanley in the back of the head. His glasses

x

12

flew off. He fell face-first into the mud.

Smash. Sherry Silverspoon stepped on Stanley's glasses with her cleats.

"Whoops," she said with an evil grin. "How clumsy of me."

"I can't see," Stanley said.

"Time out!" our coach called to the ref.

I helped my friend to his feet and started walking him over to the bench.

"You're out for the game," Coach Baloney told Stanley. "Java, you go in for him."

Oh no. Those were the last words I wanted to hear.

But Java sure seemed happy. He jogged proudly onto the field and took Stanley's defense position.

I wasn't sure what soccer skills Mom had programmed into his hard drive. Someone was going to have to teach him how to play.

"Okay, Java," I told my cousin. "Just watch me. I'll show you how this team's top scorer plays."

The ref blew his whistle. Sherry Silverspoon kicked the soccer ball high in the air. It was heading straight for our goalie, Nadine.

Uh-oh. I thought. *Here comes goal
number four.*

Java turned around and faced Nadine.

He leaped in the air.

What was he doing?

"Keep your eye on the ball, Java!" I
shouted.

Slam!

I heard the soccer ball whack Java in
the butt.

Then I watched the ball soar across the field—right over the heads of all the Red Polar Bears.

Oomf!

The ball slammed Jerry Silverspoon in the stomach.

It knocked him to the ground.

And rolled right into the net.

"**GOOOOAAAAALLLL!**" the referee shouted.

All the Purple Wombats started cheering. "Java! Java! Java!"

But *I* wasn't cheering. I was too worried.

No human butt could do something like that.

Surely someone had noticed.

I looked around.

No one on my team seemed to care *how* Java had butt-butted the ball so hard. They were just happy that he had.

The Red Polar Bears were too shocked that we had scored against them to worry about how it had happened. They just wanted to make sure it didn't happen again.

Now the Red Polar Bears were *really* ready to kick our rear ends. They got back in position for the kick-off.

So did we.

The Red Polar Bears' center forward kicked the ball. He sent it soaring across the field.

The Polar Bears raced toward our goal, ready to kick the ball right past our goalie.

Which is exactly what would have happened—if we didn't have Java.

The next thing we knew, Java was on his tiptoes, twirling around and around in a circle. Just watching him made me dizzy.

But droids don't get *dizzy*. Droids get *busy*.

Java sprung up into the air like an antelope. He did a flying ballerina split over the heads of the Red Polar Bears.

Nobody moved. We all just stood there, staring up at him.

Java landed neatly on the tips of his toes. He kicked the ball back clear across the field and right into the Red Polar Bear net.

"**GOOOOAAAAALLLL!**" the referee shouted.

All over the field, jaws dropped. Java had done it again.

Oh man. I was never going to get Java off the team now. I was going to be stuck playing soccer with him every single weekend for the rest of my life.

Or at least until it snowed. Soccer was over by then.

"Time out!" the Red Polar Bear coach shouted.

I guess he wanted a minute to figure out how his team could possibly have given up two goals in a row to the *Wombats*.

I dragged my feet to the bench to get a drink of water.

Stanley came running over. "Your cousin is the coolest!" he said.

"He just got lucky," I answered.

"Awesome job!" Stanley called over to Java.

"Thank you, Logan's friend Stanley," Java replied.

Stanley laughed.

Java looked in my direction. I turned away and walked over to the water cooler. Stanley followed me. "Why are you giving your cousin the cold shoulder?" he asked.

I opened my mouth to say something. But before I could answer, Java shouted, **"I can do it!"**

He grabbed the giant cooler filled with ice water and dumped it right onto my left shoulder.

"Ugh!" I screamed. "What did you do that for?"

Java smiled. "See? I can give you a cold shoulder, too," he said proudly.

I heard the Silverspoon twins laughing from across the field. But I didn't think it was funny.

Not one little bit.

3.

Smash!

"We are the Wombats! The winning Purple Wombats!" my teammates cheered as they carried Java on their shoulders, parading him around the pizza parlor.

"Winning Wombats!" Stanley said. "There are two words I never thought I'd hear together. It doesn't look like the Silverspoon twins ever thought they'd hear them either."

I looked across the restaurant. The Silverspoons were at a table with the rest of the Red Polar Bears. They did not look happy.

Probably because the Red Polar Bears had just lost the game 67 to 3—*to us*.

The ref had tried to end the game early. But the Silverspoon twins refused to give up.

So Java just kept on scoring.

In fact, Java had scored all sixty-seven of our Wombat goals. No one had ever run so fast or kicked so hard in the history of kid soccer.

Java was our team's high scorer now.

He was a hero. The star of our team.

He *was* our team. And everyone wanted to be around him.

I had always looked forward to soccer. I liked being the team's high scorer—even if it was on a team that lost all the time. I liked being out on the field with my friends.

But now I had to share my friends with Java. I'd never had to share anything before. It felt like my whole life was split in two.

"Java, Java, he's our man! He kicked those Bears right in the can!" cheered all the Purple Wombats.

Well, *almost* all the Purple Wombats. I wasn't in a cheering mood.

Stanley looked over at me. "What's wrong with you?" he asked. "Aren't you happy we won?"

Before I could answer, the waiter came by with a pitcher of lemonade in his hand.

"Just half a cup please," I told him.

As the waiter began to pour, Java shouted out, "**I can do it!**"

He lifted his hand and karate-chopped my glass right in half.

Lemonade spilled everywhere.

I was a sticky, gooey, yellow mess. It looked like I had peed in my pants.

"Cool!" Nadine told Java. "You must be a black belt in karate."

I groaned.

"Java! Java! He's our man! He broke that glass down with his hand!" the team cheered.

"You're so lucky to have Java for a cousin," Stanley told me. "He's like a superhero!"

A superhero? Not exactly. More like a giant, electronic, glass-smashing pain in the neck.

And who needed one of those?

4.

Slime Time!

"Hey Java! Are you ready for today's match against the Blue Chimpanzees?" Nadine asked the following Sunday, as my cousin and I walked onto the soccer field.

"*I'm* ready," I told Nadine. "Maybe I can score another goal today. Like I did that time against the Lemon-Yellow Lemurs. Remember?"

Nadine shrugged.

"Sure," she said, without even looking at me.

I didn't get it. Didn't anybody remember when *I* was the team's top scorer? It had only been a couple of weeks ago!

"You will *all* be ready, after you have chewed and swallowed my tasty snack," Java said. "It has lots of protein. My database says protein gives you energy for athletics."

"Your database?" Nadine asked.

Uh-oh.

"That's just Java's silly way of saying his brain," I said quickly.

Boy, sometimes Java could make it really hard to keep his secret.

"Oh," Nadine said with a giggle. "You're so funny, Java."

Oh brother.

"Come on, Purple Wombats," Java shouted, "try my snack!"

The whole team came running over. Java was their hero. They would do anything he said.

Java started handing sandwiches out to the team. "I made them myself," he said.

"Cool," Stanley said. He took a bite and made a face. "This tastes funny."

"What type of sandwich is this?" Nadine asked as she chewed. "It's kind of slimy."

"It's peanut butter and jellyfish," Java answered proudly.

"Peanut butter and jelly *what*?" I asked, spitting the bite of sandwich out of my mouth.

"Jellyfish," Java repeated. "According to my research, peanut butter and jelly is a favorite snack for humans."

"*Grape* jelly," I told him. "*Raspberry* jelly. *Strawberry* jelly. Not jelly*fish*. That's just gross."

"But fish helps you think better," Java said. "My database lists fish protein as—"

Bleeeccchhhhh!

Suddenly, Tom, one of our defensive players, began to puke.

Bleeeccchhhh!

Then Lexi, one of our midfielders, bent over. She started throwing up, too.

Reed, our fullback, grabbed his stomach. He started to run faster than I'd ever seen him move.

"Hey, where are you going?" I asked.

"I gotta find a bathroom—!" Reed yelled as he raced off the field.

"How are we going to play if everyone is puking their guts out?" Stanley asked Java. He sounded really upset.

"Java, why would you do this to your own team?" Tom asked angrily—right before he started puking again.

"My stomach feels like it's going to fall out," Lexi said. "What kind of a dum-dum puts jellyfish in a sandwich?"

I looked over at Java. He seemed confused, which was kind of weird for an android. I guess he didn't know he was supposed to be upset that he'd gotten everyone sick.

I felt bad for him. It wasn't fair that everyone was yelling at him.

"My cousin is no dum-dum," I said. "He just made a mistake. We can win this game. After all, we have Java on our side."

I stopped. I couldn't believe what I'd just said.

I watched as Nadine threw up a hunk of jellyfish onto the grass.

This was going to be one strange game. But Java could still win it for us.

Bleeeechhhhh. Stanley started puking.

That is, if we could make it onto the field.

5.

Something Smells Fishy

"Looks like the Purple Wombats will have to forfeit this game."

I turned around the minute I heard Jerry Silverspoon's voice. He and Sherry were standing on the sideline behind me. They looked really happy.

Which made *me* really nervous.

The Red Polar Bears weren't playing until later that afternoon. So why were the twins here now? And why were they smiling?

"Nice snack Java made for all of you," Sherry said with a nasty laugh.

"Would you like one?" Java asked her. He held up a super slimy peanut butter and jellyfish sandwich.

I rolled my eyes. Java couldn't tell Sherry was joking. But I could.

"No thanks," she told Java. "I'm not into puking."

"If you forfeit, you lose," Jerry told me. He snickered.

"And that means you stay in last place," Sherry added with a grin.

Now things were starting to make sense.

"Did *you* tell Java to make jellyfish sandwiches?" I asked the twins angrily.

"Well, the other day, Java asked us what our favorite soccer snack was," Sherry answered. She had a mean grin on her face. "I *might* have said peanut butter and jelly."

"And when he asked what kind of jelly went best with peanut butter, we *might* have listed all kinds of jelly—grape, strawberry, jelly*fish*," Jerry added, with a nasty laugh.

I should have known the twins were behind this.

"I don't know where Java comes from," Sherry said, "but I've never met anyone who didn't know how to make peanut butter and jelly."

Before I could answer, the referee called out, "Players, take the field!"

The Blue Chimpanzees all ran to their positions.

The Purple Wombats gripped their stomachs and started crawling over.

All except Java. He didn't run *or* crawl.

He shouted, **"I can do it!"**

Then he bent down and began digging up the turf. I've never seen anyone dig a hole that big, that fast before.

Java held up a pile of dirt and showed it to the ref.

"Here's the field," Java said. "Where would you like me to take it?"

Oh brother.

"That's not funny, kid," the referee said. "Put that dirt back. We have a game to play."

I looked around at my teammates. Their faces were turning all sorts of awful colors. We looked more like the *Puke-Green* Wombats.

"Java, it's all up to you," Stanley groaned as he stepped onto the field. "You're the only one who can score on the Blue Chimpanzees today."

That made me angry. I had spit out my sandwich. I wasn't sick. I could still score a goal.

I had done it once before.

But Stanley—*my best friend*—didn't think I could win the game. He was depending on Java.

I was tired of my friends thinking my

android cousin was so great.

But I didn't want the Silverspoons' evil plot to work either. No way.

"Okay, Java," I said finally. "Get scoring!"

That was all it took. My cousin became a one-man soccer machine.

He stole the ball from the Blue Chimpanzees and dribbled it down the field so fast you could barely see his feet move.

He got into position and *Slam!*

He kicked the ball right past the Chimpanzee goalie and through the net!

"**GOAAALLL!**" the ref shouted.

The Blue Chimpanzees stood there, staring.

The Purple Wombats stood there, holding their stomachs.

Tom let a little puke run out of his mouth. But he was smiling.

Our whole team was.

Java spent the whole first half slamming the ball across the field and into the Blue Chimpanzee goal.

He scored with his butt.

He scored with his feet.

He scored with his belly. There was no stopping Java.

Not that the Blue Chimpanzees didn't try. The whole team was defending against him. But Java was able to plow his way through them every time.

While the whole Blue Chimpanzee team guarded Java, I ran toward the goal.

This was my chance to score!

"Here, Java!" I shouted. "Pass it to me!"

But Java did not pass the ball to me. Instead, he kicked it hard.

Right past me.

Right past the Blue Chimpanzee's goalie.

And into the net!

"**GOOOAAALLL!**" the ref shouted again.

By now my teammates were starting to feel better. They cheered for Java.

I wasn't cheering. I could have scored.

Java just didn't give me the chance. Which wasn't fair. We're supposed to be a team.

And there's no *I* in *team*.

There's not supposed to be any *droid* in team, either. But there was one on mine.

"You're a ball hog," I shouted at my cousin.

Java gave me a funny look. "I am not a hog," he said. "I am not furry. I do not have pointy ears or a curly tail. I am a boy."

"No you're not," Stanley told Java.

Uh-oh. I looked over at my friend. Had he figured out Java's secret? This was awful. It was what I had been worried about all along.

"He's not?" I asked Stanley nervously.

"Nope," Stanley said with a smile. "He's a champion!"

Oh man.

No he's not, I thought to myself. *He's an android.*

But of course I couldn't tell Stanley that.

6.

Atomic Flush

"I've had enough!" I shouted. But no one heard me.

My mom was busy in her lab. And Java was in the backyard, chasing squirrels.

I had no idea why he was chasing them.

I didn't care either. Java could catch all the squirrels in the world. As long as he gave me my friends back.

I stormed angrily down the hall toward my room.

I couldn't believe the big deal my teammates were making over Java.

Nobody had cheered for *me* when I scored *my* goal. At least, not the way they'd cheered for Java.

"I've had enough!" I shouted even louder.

I really wanted Java off my team. I couldn't stand seeing him in that soccer jersey one more day!

I glanced over at the laundry basket sitting in the bathroom across the hall.

Java had already thrown his jersey in the basket. Which was weird, because it wasn't like it was sweaty or anything.

Androids don't sweat.

But seeing his jersey just sitting there gave me an idea.

I pulled Java's soccer jersey out of the laundry.

I threw it in the toilet.

And then I flushed.

Java's jersey swirled in the bowl. It went

around and around the drain. And then—

Water started gushing! *Everywhere.*

"Oh no!" I shouted.

Java must have heard me through the open window. The next thing I knew, he was racing up the stairs.

"What is wrong, Logan?" he asked.

I pointed at the toilet. Water was still pouring out of the bowl and onto the floor.

And not just water.

There was a goldfish.

And an old action figure.

And a baby alligator. Where did *that* come from?

"Oh man!" I cried. "I'm toast."

"**I can do it!**" Java shouted. He headed out of the bathroom and back down the stairs.

Uh-oh. What's he up to now?

Java came back right away.

"Here's your toast!" Java said, holding up a loaf of bread. "Well, it's bread anyway."

Before I could stop him, my robot cousin threw the whole loaf of bread into the toilet.

I don't know why Java did that.

Maybe he was just copying what I'd done with his jersey.

Sometimes it was nice that Java wanted to be like me.

But not now.

Whoosh! More water exploded out of the bowl.

I looked at the bathroom floor. The goldfish was swimming around my ankles.

The baby alligator was licking his chops.

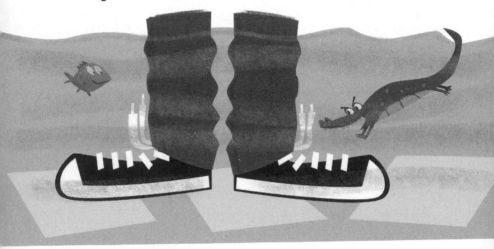

"We gotta get my mom," I told Java.

My cousin raced for the door. "I can get her," he said. "I will . . ."

Kerplonk. Java slipped on the wet floor.

Thud. He landed on his back.

Just then, I heard Mom storming up the stairs.

"What is going on in here, Logan?" she shouted.

Uh-oh. I was in trouble now.

Or maybe not.

"Java threw a loaf of bread in the toilet," I told her. "It overflowed."

That wasn't *exactly* the truth. But I figured Mom wouldn't yell at a droid for clogging the toilet.

Even if she did, Java deserved to be yelled at. He'd been a real show-off today.

"Java, why would you do that?" Mom asked him.

But Java didn't answer.

"What's wrong with him?" I asked my mom.

"I think the water short-circuited his systems," she answered.

I wasn't totally sure what that meant. But I knew for sure it was bad.

7.

Stinky-buggy-tonsil-toenail-itis

"So, were you able to order a new battery?" I asked Mom as she got off the phone a few minutes later.

"It will take about a week," Mom said. "Java needs a special battery. I had to order it all the way from Japan."

I looked over at the kitchen chair. Java was just sitting there. Without his battery he couldn't move or talk. He looked like a big toy doll.

Just then, the phone rang.

"Logan, can you answer that please?" Mom asked.

I clicked on the phone. "Hello?"

"Hi, Logan. It's Nadine."

I gulped. Nadine Vardez. Calling *my* house?

"Uh . . . hi, Nadine. Um . . . how are you?" I mumbled.

"I'm doing fine, thanks. Is Java around?"

Oh, he was around all right. *Sitting* around. Like a big, dumb rock.

But of course I couldn't say that.

"Yeah, he's here," I told Nadine. "But he can't come to the phone right now. He's um . . . kinda . . . not feeling too well."

"Oh no!" Nadine exclaimed. "Maybe I should bring him some chicken noodle soup. That will make him feel much better."

I looked over at Java. Soup was *not* going to help.

And the last thing I wanted was for Nadine to come over and see my robot cousin this way.

I had to think of something. *Quick*.

"You can't come over!" I shouted into the phone.

"Why not?"

"Java is *very* contagious. You might catch it."

"Catch what?"

"He has . . . *um* . . . stinky . . . *um* . . . buggy . . . tonsil . . . *um* . . . toenail-itis!" I blurted out.

"Stinky-buggy-tonsil-toenail-itis?" Nadine repeated. "I never heard of that."

"It's from France!" I said quickly. "He got it from eating snails."

Oh brother. I couldn't believe how dumb that sounded. Nadine would never fall for that excuse. She was too smart.

"That sounds terrible," Nadine said.

Or maybe not.

"Tell him I hope he feels better. And that we'll miss him at practice tomorrow."

Bonk.

Stanley fell face down in the mud as he tripped over the ball.

I wasn't surprised. Our whole after-school practice had been a disaster.

"That's the third time you did that, Stanley," Lexi told him. "You're supposed to *kick* the ball, not fall on it."

"No kidding," Stanley said. He spat a chunk of dirt out of his mouth. "At least I didn't knock the goal post over with my head like you did."

Our team was really a mess.

"No way we're beating those Orange Tree Frogs tomorrow without Java," Tom said to me. "Any chance he'll be better by then?"

I was getting really tired of hearing how great my cousin was.

Oomph.

Before I could answer Tom, Nadine kicked a soccer ball straight into my belly.

"Sorry, Logan," she apologized.

"That's okay," I groaned. I bent over and grabbed my stomach. "Barely felt it."

I hated to admit it, but Tom was right. We didn't have a chance.

Not without Java.

Which just made me madder. Because, deep down, I knew it was all my fault.

8.

Poor Wombats

"Ready to get your butt kicked?" Jerry Silverspoon asked me the next afternoon, right before our game against the Orange Tree Frogs.

"Because that's what's gonna happen," Sherry added with a big grin. "You're gonna lose."

The twins were all sweaty and gross.

They'd just finished playing—and beating—the Lemon-Yellow Lemurs.

But instead of going out to celebrate with their team, they were sticking around—to watch us play our game against the Orange Tree Frogs.

Or, rather, to watch us *lose* our game.

The Tree Frogs were the scariest team in the league. They were huge. And a little mean.

No one in the league could beat them. Not the Polar Bears. And certainly not us.

Without Java on our team, there was no way we could win. His battery still hadn't come to us from Japan. So there was no way *that* was happening.

"Players, take the field!" the ref called out.

For a minute I actually missed seeing Java digging up the field.

Soccer really wasn't the same without him. And not just because we couldn't win. He was actually kind of fun to be around—when he wasn't being completely annoying.

The Orange Tree Frogs ran onto the field and got ready for kickoff.

"Those kids can't be third graders," Stanley gulped. "They're *huge!*"

"They're bigger than my grandma," Tom added.

"That one has a beard," Lexi pointed out.

"So does my grandma," Tom said.

The ref blew his whistle.

The Orange Tree Frog's center forward kicked the ball all the way across the field.

Tom jumped in front of the ball. He tried to stop it. But the ball sent him flying.

Tom and the ball soared—right past
Nadine and into the goal.

"**GOOOOAAALLLL!**" the referee
shouted.

"Go Orange Tree Frogs!" Sherry
Silverspoon cheered.

"Kick their butts!" Jerry Silverspoon added.

I rolled my eyes.

This was not going to be fun.

Both teams got back in formation. Johnny, our center forward, kicked the ball toward the Orange Tree Frog goal.

Lexi and Tom both ran toward the ball.

Crash! They slammed into each other and fell to the ground in a heap.

The biggest Tree Frog stole the ball out from under them. He dribbled it back down the field.

"Stanley!" I shouted. "Steal that ball. It's coming right toward you!"

But Stanley didn't even turn around. He was busy watching a yellow and black butterfly fly over his head.

Slam! The Orange Tree Frog kicked the ball hard toward the goal.

Bam! The ball hit Stanley in the back. It knocked him over like a bowling pin.

Another Tree Frog kicked the ball toward the net. It flew right past Nadine and into the goal.

"**GOOOOAAAAALLLL!**" the referee shouted.

"Smash 'em, Tree Frogs!" Jerry cheered.

"Bash 'em, Tree Frogs!" Sherry jeered.

I couldn't even look at the twins.

The score was two to nothing. And we'd only been playing five minutes.

9.

Do the Wombat Watusi

Bam!

One of the Orange Tree Frogs kicked the ball down the field.

"Block it, Logan!" Nadine shouted from the goal cage.

I wanted to block it. But the ball was moving fast.

Faster than I could run.

Wham!

The ball slammed into the goal. Right past Nadine.

"This stinks," she groaned. "Without Java we don't stand a chance."

That made me mad.

Super duper *duper* mad.

Mostly because I knew Nadine was right. And there was nothing I could do about it.

Slowly, I headed over to the half way line. I took my spot and got ready for the kickoff.

For some reason, I started thinking about Java. He was really amazing on the soccer field.

Like that time he scored a goal with his butt.

And the time he scored a goal with his belly.

And the time he danced like a ballerina and scored against the Red Polar Bears.

That one had been *really* great.

The Polar Bears had been too shocked to try and stop him.

They had just stood there. Staring.

It had been so easy for Java to plow right past them.

Hmmm....

Just then, the ref blew his whistle.

Johnny kicked the ball.

"**I can do it!**" I shouted, suddenly.

Everyone looked in my direction.

I started cartwheeling down the field.

I did a forward roll. And leaped up onto my toes.

Then I began swinging my hips back and forth and waving my arms up and down.

"Logan," Tom shouted. "What are you doing?"

"The watusi," I answered.

I wiggled my hips harder. I waved my arms higher.

"Do the wah-wah-watusi!" I sang as I wiggled and waved.

The Orange Tree Frogs all stood there, staring at me with their mouths wide open.

"Logan, you're a weirdo," Jerry Silverspoon shouted from the stands.

"A wiggling, waving, *watusi* weirdo," Sherry added.

But I didn't care. I just kept wiggling. And waving.

Everyone was watching me dance.

Everyone except Stanley, that is.

He was busy watching a bunch of ants pile out of an anthill by his feet.

That was a problem. *Because the ball was coming right to him.*

"Stanley!" I shouted. "Get the ball! Take it down the field!"

He looked up suddenly. "Huh?"

"The ball!" I shouted again. I pointed at his feet.

Stanley looked down at the ball.

He kicked it. Then he kicked it again.

The next thing anyone knew, Stanley was racing down the field, dribbling the ball.

The Orange Tree Frogs could have stopped him.

They *should* have stopped him.

But they didn't.

They were so busy watching me watusi they didn't even notice Stanley.

I wiggled my hips harder.

I waved my arms wider.

"Do the wah-wah-watusi!" I sang out again.

Stanley kept running.

Past the Tree Frog forwards.

And their midfielders.

And their defenders.

And then . . .

Slam!

GOOOAAAALLLL!

"**GOOOAAAALLLL!**" the referee shouted.

Yes! Stanley had scored.

Okay, it was only one goal.

But at least the Wombats were on the scoreboard.

10.

Come Clean

Stanley sure was happy.

We might have lost the game. But he had scored for the first time in his life.

I knew I was the real reason Stanley had scored. But I didn't say that. I didn't want to hurt his feelings.

Besides, it really didn't matter *who* scored. We were part of a team.

When I got home I went upstairs to take off my cleats and soccer jersey.

Mom was in the bathroom, fixing the toilet. *Again*. It was still overflowing every time we flushed.

"Hi, Logan," Mom called to me. "How did the game go?"

"We lost."

"I'm sorry," Mom replied.

"It's okay," I said. "Maybe we'll win next time. Do you think Java will be ready to play soon?"

"Sure," Mom answered. "His new battery came this afternoon."

Phew. That was a relief.

"Oh, and I programmed him to not drop bread or any other weird objects down the toilet."

Just then, Java walked by.

I looked down at my shoes. I felt really bad about blaming Java for stuffing up the toilet.

"Mom, I've got to come clean about something. I—"

But before I could tell her the truth, Java shouted, **"I can do it!"**

He raced into the bathroom, grabbed a bar of soap, and started rubbing it under his pits.

"I can come clean, too," he said.

"That's not what I meant," I told him. "I wanted to say that I tried to flush your soccer jersey down the toilet. That was what really stuffed it up. I'm sorry."

Mom gave me a funny look.

Uh-oh. I was in trouble now.

She reached out and gave me a big

hug.

Okay, I was *definitely* not expecting that!

I was kind of expecting to be grounded.

"I'm really proud you told the truth," Mom said.

Phew.

"And by the way, you're grounded," she added.

That was more like it.

"I can do it!" Java shouted out suddenly. He shoved me to the floor, hard.

I landed right on my butt.

"See, Logan?" Java said proudly. "Now you are on the ground. *Grounded.*"

Mom laughed.

But I didn't think it was so funny.

I rubbed my rear end. That hurt.

Still, I guess I kind of deserved it. I

hadn't been very nice to Java lately.

I was just going to have to get used to the idea that sometimes I was going to be the best. But sometimes my robot cousin was going to be the one to come out on top.

That's just the way it is in a family.

And when it came to soccer, Java was the top dog—er—*droid*.

I rubbed my aching backside again.

I definitely had a sore butt.

But, hey, at least I wasn't a sore loser.

There's a Soccer Ball on the Ceiling!

Logan learned the hard way that flushing a soccer jersey is a really, really, really bad idea. Some things just don't belong in the toilet.

Like jerseys. Or action figures. Or alligators. A lot of things don't belong hanging from your *ceiling*, either. Luckily, a soccer ball isn't one of them.

In fact, you can hang a soccer ball from your ceiling anytime you want—as long as it's a super soccer ball lantern you've made all by yourself.

93

Here's what you'll need:

- ⚙ 1 white paper lantern that is 20 inches in diameter
- ⚙ 4 sheets of tissue paper in the color of your favorite soccer team
- ⚙ Scissors
- ⚙ Cardboard
- ⚙ Mod Podge® with a glossy finish
- ⚙ 1 paintbrush
- ⚙ 1 soccer ball (to use as a model)
- ⚙ An adult to help you

Tissue paper

Scissors

Lantern

Soccer ball

Paintbrush

Adult

Cardboard

Mod Podge®

Here's what you do:

1 Ask your helpful adult to cut a pentagon-shaped template out of the cardboard. (A pentagon is a shape with five equal sides.) The pentagon template should be cut to be the same size as the black pentagons on your real soccer ball.

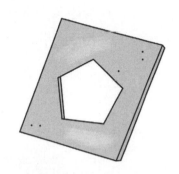

2 Use the template to cut twenty pentagons from the tissue paper.

3 Use the paintbrush to paint a little spot of Mod Podge® on each tissue paper pentagon, and gently stick it to your paper lantern.

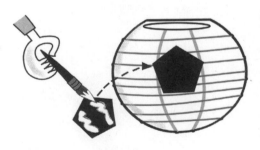

4 Repeat Step 3 twenty times, until all of the pentagons are stuck to the lantern. Try to copy the pattern the black pentagons make on your real soccer ball.

95

5 Paint a light coat of Mod Podge® over each pentagon to seal it completely onto your paper lantern.

6 Allow your lantern to dry.

7 Ask your helpful adult to hang your new soccer ball lantern from your ceiling.

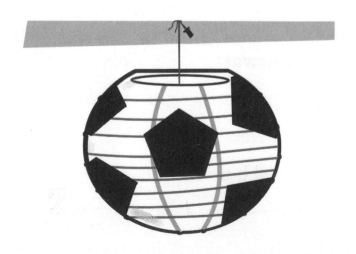

About the Authors

Nancy Krulik is the author of more than two hundred books for children and young adults including three *New York Times* bestsellers and the popular Katie Kazoo, Switcheroo; George Brown, Class Clown; and Magic Bone series. She lives in New York City with her husband and crazy beagle mix. Vist her online at www.realnancykrulik.com

Amanda Burwasser holds a BFA with honors in creative writing from Pratt Institute in New York City. Her senior thesis earned her the coveted Pratt Circle Award. A preschool teacher, she resides in Santa Rosa, California.

About the Illustrator

Mike Moran is a dad, husband, and illustrator. His illustrations can be seen in children's books, animation, magazines, games, World Series programs, and more. He lives in Florham Park, New Jersey. Visit him online at www.mikemoran.net